To Meryl,

1/14/11

Elmer the Dog

Special thanks to Vuthy,
without whom this never could have happened.

Also, special thanks to Jean Oliver for her hard work.

The author is also grateful for his Mom and Dad,
as well as his friends Keri, Peter, Wendy, Adam, Gretchen,
Ed, Dana and all those folks at TTP.

And of course, a certain real-life Elmer the Dog.

Published by Providence Publishing (888)966.3833
4306 Brook Woods, Houston, TX 77092
Printed in China through Morris Press Ltd
Fourth Printing 10 9 8 7 6 5

Library of Congress Catalog Card Number 99 097228
Nguyen, Duke; Kuon, Vuthy, Elmer the Dog
Summary: A story of a dog who learns that what makes
him different is also what makes him special.
ISBN 0-9675803-0-7

Elmer the Dog

Written by Duke Nguyen

Illustrated by Vuthy Kuon

Edited by Alysia Gonzalez

& Lavaille Lavette

BROWN DOG PRESS

an imprint of Providence Publishing

Once there was a dog named Elmer.

Elmer was a normal little puppy, who liked little puppy things, like chew toys, balls, swimming and large T-bone steaks drowned in Teriyaki sauce.

His mom, GlorieBell, was a prize-winning Labrador Retriever.
"There's nothing like a good stick!" she'd always say.

Elmer's dad was a blue-blooded pure-bred German Short Haired Pointer. His name was Axel and he liked to tell Elmer, "There's no better way to spend a day than sniffing!"

Naturally, GlorieBell and Axel wanted Elmer to grow up to be a good dog. So they sent him to school, Donnie Laredo's Super Dog Obedience School.

"That's where the best and brightest dogs go!" said GlorieBell.

"Then that's where our Elmer will go!" said Axel.

And so to Donnie Laredo's Super Dog Obedience School Elmer went. There were all kinds of puppies there. Labrador Retrievers like his mom. German Short Haired Pointers like his dad. Plus, all kinds of other dogs like Collies, Poodles, Saint Bernards, Boxers and Beagles. But the thing about all of them was that, unlike Elmer, they were pure breeds.

Which means Poodles had Poodles for parents, Collies had Collies for parents, and so on.

"We are pure breeds," the dogs would say. "Here are our papers, can't you see? Our stock is as pure as pure as can be!"

"Where are *your* papers?" a poodle with a pink ribbon in her hair asked Elmer.

"Papers? What do you mean papers?" said Elmer. "Why do I need paper? Are we taking notes already?"

The poodle smirked and her pooch friends giggled, "Why no you silly dog! We mean your breeding papers, to say you are a pure breed. Say, what are you?"

Elmer answered, "My mom is a Labrador Retriever and my dad is a German Short Haired Pointer."

The dogs gasped. One of them, possibly the Great Dane, cried out, "Why he's nothing more than a mutt!"

The pure breeds were horrified. A mutt in their midst? How could it be? They didn't want anything to do with Elmer. And poor Elmer, he was so upset he messed up ALL his assignments. He even "sat" when he was supposed to "roll over." How embarassing!

When Elmer got home from obedience school he howled,
"*Woooo! Woooooo!*" Then he said, "I don't like school!
I don't want to go back. Ever!"

GlorieBell was so shocked, she dropped her stick.
"Why, what happened Elmer?"

"The other dogs, they're all pure breeds,"
sniffled a sad Elmer.
"I'm nothing but a mutt!"

"Just a mutt? Goodness gracious!"
said Axel.

GlorieBell took Elmer in her paws and said, "Oh silly Elmer, being a mixed breed isn't a bad thing. It's a gift!"

"A gift?" said Elmer.

"Of course," answered Axel, "having two different kinds of parents means you are blessed with two different sets of abilities. It's the best of two worlds!"

"You have all the talents of a Labrador," said Elmer's mom.

"Plus, all the skills of a Pointer!" added Elmer's dad.

Elmer hugged his mom and dad. They licked Elmer all over his face until he felt better.

The next day at school the dogs were not any nicer. But Elmer remembered his parents' words when it came time to retrieve sticks. He told himself, "I'm half Labrador Retriever, and Labs are great at fetching sticks. I bet I can do it too!" And he could. He finished in the top group.

"Hmmph, beginners luck," complained a Beagle.

But it wasn't.

Because with all the talents of a German Short Haired Pointer and all the abilities of a Labrador Retriever, there were few things Elmer was not good at.

Slowly but surely, as the Terriers sank in the swimming pool, the Boxers sniffed in all the wrong places and the Saint Bernards passed out on the track, Elmer did better and better.

When the end of the day rolled around, only Elmer
had finished in the top of every group. He even got
an "Official Donnie Laredo Medal of Excellence!"

As for the other dogs, they changed their tune
about their mixed breed classmate.

"You're such a talent!" said a Poodle.

"An absolute marvel," added the Cocker Spaniel.

"Will you sign my collar?" begged the Saint Bernard.

When Elmer got home he burst in the door and exclaimed with glee, "Mom! Dad! School was *dog-gone* great! I made the top group every time. And I even got a medal!"

"That's my boy!" barked Elmer's dad.

GlorieBell hugged Elmer and asked him, "So, you're not sad to be a mutt anymore?"

"Oh, of course not!" said Elmer.

That night Elmer and his parents had
a party to celebrate his big day. It
was *woof-woof* wonderful!